SKATE FATE

JUAN FELIPE HERRERA

SKATE FATE

AN IMPRINT OF HARPERCOLLINS*PUBLISHERS*

Rayo is an imprint of HarperCollins Publishers.

SkateFate

For information address HarperCollins Children's Books, a division of HarperCollins Publishers, 10 East 53rd Street, New York, NY 10022.

www.harperteen.com

Library of Congress Cataloging-in-Publication Data
Herrera, Juan Felipe.
Skatefate / Juan Felipe Herrera. — 1st ed.
p. cm.
Summary: Lucky Z, a Chicano foster child, loved living on the edge until a drag racing accident left him in a wheelchair, but as he struggles to find his place in a new high school, he begins writing poetry everywhere about anything, and in finding his voice he also discovers the beauty around him.
ISBN 978-0-06-143287-3
[1. Novels in verse. 2. Poets—Fiction. 3. People with disabilities—Fiction. 4. High schools—Fiction. 5. Schools—Fiction. 6. Foster home care—Fiction. 7. Moving, Household—Fiction. 8. Mexican Americans—Fiction.] I. Title.
PZ7.5.H466Sk 2011 2010014974
[Fic]—dc22 CIP
AC

Typography by Andrea Vandergrift
11 12 13 14 15 LP/RRDB 10 9 8 7 6 5 4 3 2 1

First Edition

For Lawrence King

A fifteen-year-old middle school boy from Oxnard, California,

who was shot and killed by another student

for what prosecutors said was a hate crime.

A few weeks before the incident, Lawrence's classmates said

that he had publicly declared that he was gay.

Rest in Power, Lawrence.

And

For all the boys who love the color pink.

. . . LET US GO FORTH
IN THE BOLD DAY,
AND WRITE.

—Walt Whitman, "Proud Music of the Storm,"
from *Leaves of Grass*

LUCKY Z'S JOURNAL

boom-blam that was the last thing i heard.
a so forever scream slid through me
Is this a dream Lucky i asked myself

just rolled here new foster parents new streets.
new beats. new kids laughing out loud so what if i
wear fruity tops skinny black pants so what if i sing
to myself so what if i write in a hot-pink journal
so what if i drag tons of art and poetry books.
Levertov. Baudelaire. Van Gogh. Whitman.
Neruda. Chagall. Passolini. hear me. Mattie
Stepanek is my favorite. cuz he wrote poems sitting
in his wheelchair breathing through a tube in his
throat. scribbled them as fast as he could for everyone. yeah like that. that's what it's all about dude

i was saying this over and over to Klarissa my new
cool friend before it all happened. Jason Blocker
was after me. said You never gonna be in the Scene
girly. and you are never gonna really ever skate.
you're sooo gay! read this i told him. here. get a grip.
winked at him. heh

THIS MORNING

I HEAR

MYSELF

SINGING

i hear myself singing
a clear morning a sun filled with laughter
everything that everyone is after right here
inside my song this iTune i am on this *melodía* i am ringing
bounce from the mirror bounce from the flower
in my foster mother's short hair here & there or now or
some day never i say Now i hear myself
not yesterday when i was sad
alone under the shade of a broom in my hip-hop room
my father somewhere somewhere saying when you have life
well—be alive! At 2 or 7 or 6 or 11!
there is no clock when your voice rises & trembles an iris
on the fence or the dock each petal curled up
around the world each other around each color never settle
for the cold iron gray of a bullet-riddled metal pinging
open your heart that's how i start
a clear morning a sun filled with laughter
everything that everyone is after happens now
i hear myself singing singing

ACROSS THE STREET AT THE GREEN SPEEDWAY CAFÉ

valedictorian cannoli
wrapped so elegantly on a neon city tray
here i come come
madame hip-hop powder puff
mademoiselle éclair may i
sit at your side
on this wheely black-strap trickster chair
please please
one fiery cappuccino tease
one strawberry shortcake awake & those crunchy
wait! what is this on my iPod nano?
my grandmother Serafina's border ballads from afar?
papa z's desperate gypsy beats from the war?
shall we skateboard
on this delirious apple-shaped floor?
clap for a night of nutmeg
& cinnamon dancers
clap for the answers in chocolate autumn-leaf dresses
barefoot blushed cheeks hot-hot Milky-Way breath
oh the rest is on my long blackish hair—clap!

INSIDE MY PENCIL BOX

number two lead

skinny gummy toothpick poles the color of tar

punky eraser with a bony shaved head

who wants to write about Manitoba Trout sooo far?

yellow beads sunflower seeds & a bee's head without a tie

soggy crumbs taste *mm-mmmm* good

from last year's pumpkin pie

ON THE PALM TREE

STANDING
TALL
BEFORE ME

tiny rough childhoods

roots bent astray

songs of night

starry children

hidden seeds

lost embraces

scattered hearts and gone faces

one

by one

flowerings

going into

red-brown going into

fire fawn traces

breathe for us

rise *for us*

newborn harmonies

shimmerings

glimmerings

lingering

boy of spiked

strands & girl of

roaring tides

wild fruits &

dark-petaled eyes

i bow to you

ON MY METROCARD

jot down 5 things

that i can balance on my forearm

jot down 9 things

that when splashed together look

like the earth

jot down 17 things

that rhyme with Thyme

jot down 3 easy streets

for foster girl fights

jot down 9 words

that i know are 100% magic

jot down the word *Lost*

& stretch it into *Most*

ON THE LAST MIDNIGHT DRAG RACE

ON A STREET NAMED DESIRÉE

for your open shirt fender that flies

for fragments of bittersweet mags & tags & a sigh

for your violet-brushed eyelash & your crazy single i

that crashes when light sings alone

for your dive drive into the pale street's gasoline moon

to burnish to flow to attract the sun

for your hand this multiplied fan

these shatters of Pluto & Venus out of orbit

for your cosmic engine sassy brain colliding

flashing conspiring messages dashing against themselves

for your siren voice your hollering

night shout fright trapped locked door

for your face where is it what was it

half this half that with this without that

for your heart all i have

this skate that churns metal flake blues & burns burns

hear

your last midnight drag race voice calling me back:

Don't race me now don't race me now

cuz i am g o n e

ON THE

GIRL TREE

STRUCK BY

LIGHTNING

IN THE

MIDDLE

OF

NOWHERE

in black all black
without branches or
friends or fears or anything near

in brown & sepia music
in blue nest nothingness
absolute singular & cut to glass
transformed into light & sky & void
realized—all
possible knowing & unknowing
motionless measureless in shards
struck spliced delivered
charred blond peel
leaf without water or substance
or blood or back to behold

Stand you
stand

I SING TO
MYSELF
AT THE CURB
BEFORE
I TAKE
ANOTHER
STEP

why are you singing under the saucy sun
the blurry skylight of all things
why are you trembling there
with a torn foot & a messy rain jacket
why are you waving your hands grabbing stars from afar
you! yes, you!
why are you breathing rough & starin' up
& rasping your boot
why are you nervous & jazzy & crazy & brassy & quiet too
why are reading your own rhymes & spittin' out the words
no one is here!
why is it you & just the sky-eye the air the flare
of clouds & the street
why is all this concrete beat to you a galaxy to you a song
to you, yes, you!
why don't you have an answer Why you ask then you say

AT THE GO-GO GIFT SHOPPE

for the computer tech nerd—

licorice sticks tangled up into algebra

& a greasy skateboard losing it electric

for the seventeen & a half year old test-driving
a new speedy ride—

crazy-glue gloves from Daytona

no-stick bubble gum & no-sweat socks

for all the Iraq vets in the hospital waiting room—

fluffy free ice cream &

a Tchaikovsky sky symphony swoon

Lucky Klarissa said Maybe you should work on fitting in dude you look like a weird wild Mexican cowboy. some kinda mariachi in a painted Gaga shirt and those oh ma-gosh gnarly twig pants and funky lizard boots dude! but cowboys don't have a red-pink faux-hawk boiling up from their cabeza right. plus a wheelchair that says Out & About. grinned back snappin' my pencil box. breathing mellow smoothing the bumpy scar on my forehead

got a steel rod in my back. and screws all up my left leg. right leg paralyzed. it happened after my father came back from Iraq three years ago started talking to himself in his room. talkin' in beeps. exclamations. no subjects. no objects. explosions. like he was being attacked by crazy commas from across the ocean. blasts and stuttering bullets going nowhere. until nothing but gasps. poor papa. then he left my mama. it all happened after my mother died from breast cancer a year later and after i drag-raced into the night with Sammy Valencia and Des Nguyen loaded on crystal yeah Des didn't make it ahhh dunno. she was so cool

and tuff always crackin' up that was two years ago
and two years of therapy. and cryin' stuff into this
journal. nothin' but cryin' dude you'd think i was
Niagara Falls. yup

ON THE WINDY ROAD TO SCHOOL

UNDER
THE
CARNATION CROSS
THREADED
ONTO MY
SCHOOL
FENCE

paper carnations
    on my high school fence
any town any street but   not just
  anyone
      today the sunlight speaks
    candles lit at noon
  by the cafeteria she sneaks
reaches   for you
a row of postcards exhale pink ink
      teddy bear sleeps
        love love breath breath
  in & out—now i know
a paper carnation can live forever
  a 12th grade name remains—
    Desirée yesterday
      at the assembly on Careers
  your face   still silky—
      hold her   in your hands
    carry her for a moment wind
  singsingsing

ROUND THE CROSSWALK RAILS

stroll
under the trees
they bend
they send messages in autumn
from Desirée's red-ribboned hair
a leaf

falls

ON THE SCHOOL SECURITY ENTRANCE GATE SCANNER

scan my loose snarl jacket zipper

but you don't see my gone mother angel warrior

memory picture

scan my belt chrome diamonds my death skull T of slang

fang nations

but you don't see my shatter street drag-race howl

glass constellations

scan my wheelchair ride flyin' fast faster than Einstein's

gamma rays

but you don't see my ragged race to a nowhere

comin' home place

scan me scan me scan all of me

if you can

ON AN EMPANADA APPLE TURNOVER BEHIND THE LUNCH LINE

you baked me
you raked me
you pinched me

you cinnamon-danced me
you oven-placed me
you flour-tossed me

then you let me cool
you tall handsome fool

ON MY CRAZZZY COOL FRIEND ROKERO'S LOCKER

yo'

Mop & Glow

you with that half-punky Mexicano shave kit

think you are all that

famous now huhuh

Timberlands as wide as Miami dude

& i can hear your BiGsOWaZUp

still wearin' yo' Columbine trench sooo fried soooo

craaaaaaZeeeeee

hey

YouStinK

jeskiddin-hah

thass why i can hang wit you

youstandinup 4 me & all

timez up

are you widit

yaKnow . . . U&Me

senioryear is herelikeyeah

soooWhaaat

you gonnaDoooooooooooooo?

AT THE CHOIR REHEARSAL SESSION

Mr. Ezra Harrison Maxwell in his white Calvin Klein shirt
halts Florante Sarmiento's piano cantata by Bach
pulls me over—says
listen-listen
you are a new tenor here & you have a beautiful voice but
you are only using one third of it—

1/3
of it?

HANG

IT ON

ALYTTA'S

EARRINGS

I SAY

cha-cha *cha*
cha-cha-cha *oh*

cha-cha *me?*
cha *oh*

cha- *hello*
cha-cha-cha *me*

cha-cha *&*

you?

oucha-cha-cha

ON MY POMEGRANATE-COLORED CELL: TEXTMESSAGE #10030027655

textmetextmetextme

textmetextmetextme

textmetextmetextme

textmetextmetextme

textmetextmetextme

textmetextmetextme

textmetextmetextme

textmetextmetextme   Winter   & i

willtextyoutextyoutextyoutextyoutextyoutextyoutextyoutext

U

S u mmm e r

ON

A

LAPTOP

SPACE BAR

(4TH PERIOD)

touch me again dude & i'll cursor you

ON SEKOU'S
HIP-HOP HAT
FLOATING UP
TO THE
ELECTRIC
LIGHT BLUE

toss me through the cosmic waves
toss me through the broken sky-floor
toss me until you see me no more
toss me as far as your arm can
toss me with your heart not your hand
toss me into the undiscovered delight
toss me into your velvet night
toss me without time or thought or might
toss me without getting caught
toss me with your own birth-born wealth
toss me just like that—like that
& i'll flip back
right on your own magical forever self

ON RONISHA'S CELL (PEARL BLACK)

hey waZup wait wait ahA wait now now what wait
did you say aHa wait my cell oh well oH
aha my cell wait oK Ok ok now where was
i wait hold Up i'll be there i am almost there
aha now wait hUh what she she she wANTS him?
you gender-confused? my cell's breaking up again
& you were like DuH and she was like DuDE
whaT yOu want him tOo wait thatz way uncOO
whatwhat? you are Over dude what did you say
ok ok where was i don't crY aha Yeah right like
i am like totally like wHat? dude! like hey stiLL there?

DEEP INSIDE

BRYCE'S

MINIATURE

CHERRY BLACK

BACKPACK

ON HER

BACK

Is it a boy? *¿Será un niño?*

Is it a girl? *¿Será una niña?*

Is it the end of the world? *¿Será el fin fin del mundo?*

AT THE GO-GO GIFT SHOPPE

for all security personnel—

John Lennon psychedelic motorized glasses &

marshmallow periscope baseball hats

for the new boy in a wheelchair—

roller coasters made of laughter &

an emerald green soccer field

for the career counselor meany on the 2nd floor—

an enchilada tray wrapped carefully & correctly

with cuckoo confetti & firecracker snot-balls inside

gotta new thing can't describe it. i fly around
Pacifico school putting out my poems
wherever i go yeah it's like that now. seriously.
can still skate around but on two pizza-sized wheels
ha. crazy huh. like i am totally into spittin' it all
out yeah. that's what i was saying to Klarissa Green
and her teddy bear when Jason popped the door

IN THE DUSTY AFTERNOON

SKATE IT UNDER THE SUN

skate it under the fire
of that ancient-bearded goddess—fierce
carved
alive
on the sands burning infinite without a name
in each shivery uncertain & unknowable grain
in
your
hands

SKATE IT ON ALL THE LONELY CASAS

on all the sunburned houses & all the rooms
        & all the perfumes
on the nurses hats & junior leagues at bat
on the hospital light & the evening rush melting
            under a school
on the disappearing street of purple smoke
            & the license plate
on the big foster sister's shoulder getting home late
            on the chip chips
falling from trees & kitchen walls & gasoline stalls &
abandoned scenes & crumbling movie theater screens
all the greens of all the leaves of all the trees
    on all the *sí*'s & yes's
& all the dresses that each season brings

ON THE HANDS

OF ALL

THE HOMELESS

FATHERS

&

THE HOMELESS

MOTHERS

&

THE HOMELESS CHILDREN PAINTED IN STREETLIGHT YELLOW

as you fumble on a fancy corner of decorations & signs
about modern times
as you scratch your scalp when i ask
the question about hunger
as you peer into my eyes with rivers lost & fires scattered
as you grow quiet in the traffic tumbling in all directions
at the same time
as you let your faces water under the wacked furious sun
as you touch a little photo of a girl curly-haired
pinned to your Lakers jacket
as you play with faceless buttons rust wrenches
pages & pages of nothing
as you bend toward me speechless
as if i was your lost Lady Gaga
as you resemble the scars of your belly your legs
your ankles your feet
as you run & run & run & run away from me
with your plastic bags in knots
as you shake & offer me a blue black newspaper
that no one reads

as you salute me magical royal kinky shredded & prophetic
as you clutch dolls a golden dog a sparrow
& pillows with tiny flowers
as you open your hands asking for words why am i here &
you are there

ON THE METRO-LINK SEAT

sit read please

latest blackwhite

newspaper

say something to

freckled Robin chromey starry braces

something cool come on

somesomething coo-cool

likelikelikelikelike

the Democratic Arctic

is melting & . . .

likelikelikelikelikelikelike

the Republican pelican brief

is full of flamingo seed . . .

say

something *romántico*

to the fuchsia lip gloss

babeyeah

likelikelikelikelikelikelikelike

ON MY

PINK

PLAIN

CHUCKS

jot 3 words that begin with a Z like Zacarías
jot 5 cities that start with an A as in Anywherebuthere
jot 7 things i will do when i graduate out loud
jot 100 things i can make with a to-go cup
jot 21 hearts i can draw on my arm
jot 1 haunting love rhyme i can hang on a drifting cloud

ON A SUPERMARKET GROCERY RECEIPT

dead tomatoes .25 cents?
two mysterious violet & poetic eggplants
aisle number 99 next to the detergent
why is this sooo urgent?
someone tell me hey mister
my iPod i lost it under the jalapeños
forgot everything
they don't make tortillas
the way they used to holy holy holy!
what happened to the eggs?
they all feel the same
hey Whitman i am lost so lost
the watermelons are licking
their wounds ah heavenly
okay there's the lemonade
i found the lemonade Hey
everybody i found the lemon—

IN BETWEEN MY FOSTER CASA & THE HARD WORLD

where the sun is still watery

whimpery soft & uncurled

where the alley night appears

as a yoke of tawny smoke

where each dreamy footstep glows

on the powderpowder sands

where half of me cartwheels

on the whirly foothills

where the other half breaks out

into elastic planets

where me & you & me & you

gossip a little about us two

where guns & knives & bombs & needles & bullies

are loomingboomingzooming

where hearts & minds & sometimes

kindness & time & time & time

seem so so far away

AT THE GO-GO GIFT SHOPPE

for the nurse—

Pepto apples & Alka pears

for the firefighter—

watermelon hats & diamond fountains

for the little girl on the dentist's leather & chrome chair—

iced white chocolate mocha lattes &

a furious-fast candy-apple colored limo

Jason Blocker's hand came up to me with a
silver lightning flower at the end of it. opened
up and grew so fat it ripped everything out of the
classroom. dunno. just heard myself stutterin'.
somewhere. in middle of the. blast

UNDER THE WET STARS

SKATE IT
ON A KITE
AT NIGHT

send it to the stars
send it to the stars

when they tremble
eon dresses in light-year skies
grandmother Serafina's bedroom curtains rise
light up in amber sighs

ON A BROKEN-UP STRAWBERRY-COLORED SKATER DOLL

on the gnarled foot so it will turn into a swan
on the hurt breast so that every beat of the heart
  writes a new word for love
on the shattered hip so that the consonants
        become cha-cha-chas
on the screwed fingers so that new vowels
                without the howls sprinkle out & grow
on the twisted head so that colors wind sail & pigtail
                        into laughing skies
on the ripped belly so that every building bends at the center
                                & bows to you
on the split knees so you can climb beyond Mercury
                                        beyond Beyond
on the aching ankles so that every other sour shoe
                                can become skippery-sugary
on the reddish palm so that every no no no will now know
                            how to glow

ON THE TAG

ON PAPA Z'S

DUFFEL BAG

AT THE LAST

GREYHOUND STATION

war

is not

a video

game

war is not a video game papa z tells me

but sometimes i think it is all the same

SKATE IT
INSIDE A
RAINDROP

so when it falls
on the frozen windshield without notice
the glass will melt &
spell your name in one wavy Alaskan blast
when the driver ambles in & tosses the worker jacket
the tennis racket & all that world affairs racket
her eyes will read you through the shifting ice
balanced in the air all that is there
every moment born anew at last

IF YOU FIND A POEM BEFORE YOU GO TO BED

if you find a wet drippy poem

a poem filled with goldfish splashing Jupiter colors on a dish

or

a poem of tadpoles skipping over a tuna

making a whale of a wish

if you find a marvelous majestic mellifluous poem

that wants to sing

tired & tied to a 8 1/2 x 11-inch white picket fence paper

untie it—that is all &

take a rubber-band taper from the morning paper

& tape it to the wind for goodnesssaker & let it become

Spring

AT THE GO-GO GIFT SHOPPE

for the astronaut—

a mailbox of tangerine horizons & two trillion tortillas

flapping around Saturn

for mad foster moms driving you to school—

Capezios to make it all easy-os &

a hooray Hula dancing class at twelve o'clock

for the faux-hawk skater cruisin' to the stars—

coconut-flavored Post-its & a swimming pool filled with 7Up

now i can talk about it. after a year of screws in my legs and operations and tubes swishin' in and out of my stomach and kidneys i just wanted to roar out. touch things i had never touched. to see if it was true. was i still here was this life still here. on this side. whatever you call it dude. wanted to touch everything like van Gogh touched and smeared everything when he painted. so i wrote it and spoke it. maybe mama would hear me. cuz i could hear her. sayin' When your heart hurts sing. wherever you go. and i'll be there. maybe Des would surprise me parked around the corner. maybe papa would come back. sometimes in between the commas and periods and semicolons and gasps he said things to me. he said. Lucky. i. love. you.

THIS
MORNING

ON MY SKATEBOARD

porpoisenosed

cheetahpawed

ancestralfinfinfin

bluequiverriversilvers

sawdust of awesome awe

here

i

gooooooooooooooooo!

gooooooo!

gooooooooooo!

goooooooo!

goooooooo!

when you are dreaming you are dreaming
that is when you are awake when
French violet flower petals greet you like van Gogh &
all the streets lead to where you are
& there is no where to go you know you know
blue green hills & dawny-light & hope fill your eyes &
shake your heart
when the A train rides you to the City of Sparkles
& you call out
"here's where i stop so i can start!"
when each finger paints & each breath almost faints
all the moony messages & sassy singers
from all the fire escapes fly out it's your turn! they shout
it's your time! they dance
it's your rhyme! it's your chance
in a circle made of infinite circles in a breath
that breathes all our breath
when your face is smeared with summer & winter
autumn & spring sorrow & laughter what you lost
& what you are after what is soaring &
what sails under the sea
your season is here you see

it is near
can you hear its freedom melody ringing

it is you
so skate a poem
wherever you go & you & all will know

you
can be tragic you can
be casual & usual & unusual
1,2,3 put a poem on backward
& it starts to spell Me

are you listening-listening
write it weak every week
write it strong so every line can goooooooo
looooooooooooooooooong &
belong
to your unexpected song

that's it
that's it—4, 5, 6, 7, 8, i said nine
print it on an Abercrombie sign
a BMX flying over Spider-Man bouncing sticky
across time right in the skate-skate it right there with a flair

right there

for all the looooosers & all the wiiiiiiiinners

for those grounded for all those wounded

in wars at home in the school yard unknown

in wars far away in wars no one can say You're so gay

when all is quiet in the foster home zone

when every face & space in MySpace quivers &

logs out for a thrilli-second of rhyme

skate a poem that is your cue your sign

wherever you go

in a flurry in a hurry a textmessage w/o a worry

text it there text it in your own

magnificent mysterious texteriousway

text it to the girl with wrists cut

whose father storms into her room with the dust of Iraq

gone so soon?

text it to the boy with his mother so poor so lost under

the liquor light moon

text it to the girl-boy considering the angry gnarly rope cool

hanging from the roof so solemn so hairy so early in

that lonely shadow pool

text it to the teen soldier

ten years older
than yesterday's improvised explosive device duel
get serious with it seriously
get delirious with it deliriously
get omnivorous with it omnivorously
¡opalescentplasmathunderquake!
ithappenedtome
when i went flyin' & cryin' & dyin'
for goodness sake i ain't lying
be with it

be in it

be for it & after it beeeeeeeeeeeeeeeeeeeeeee
the poem thass all
be the song-song
you are singing
with ADD or
stutter-free with acne & ghee & horchata on your knee
with a bow-legged shape
with crisscross eyes that can truly see
with busted legs the color of eggs

with freckles & dimples &

heckles & Shrek-colored me's

going

going

gooooing

further than your dreams & screams

invisible & visible & visualized & televised

in your high-def lows &

your diggable-digital highs

in the eyelash of hip-hop creation or

in the woo-whoo of your own Claymation imagination

skate a poem there

do it pronto

for your girlfriend

for your self-fried

for your boywhocried

skate a poem crazy & lazy & wiggly & wobbly & brave

ready—i said go!

skate a poem wherever you goooooooooooooooooooooo

blog it

pog it

ride it

roo it

goo it

do it

crew it

brew it

shoo it

shoe it

moo it

blue it

Sue it

froo-fruit it

10, 11, 12, 13, 14, 15, 16, 17, eighteen

OMG—

skate it

on all the things

that come from no things in sight & things

critically wrong complicated fragile & magnificently strong

deodorant-stick fried burritos Bengal tiger carpet that's

where your pet went

dental braces & Disney gongs & throngs of

pregnancy tests & physics books & dental floss

Goth shoes plain white laces

quadratic formula prep-test races

isosceles triangles &

número dos basketball championship shoes
what do you want Baghdad or divorce?
no one asked you to choose
diet obsessions behavioral mess any
more crunchy questions anyone
adoption option & foster papers all that mess you wished
was gone
PennySaver & craigslist gone wrong
you don't know what kind of boy you are or you aren't
skate it there girl or boy or both whatever
vitamin water or the fume in the perfume market crash &
all the rash
on your ex-friend takin' a lap & then a nap
in between all the gangsta' rap no fear
on CNN on all the baby names
on your stepmom's *Grey's Anatomy* at night
on the boy with the gun in the gloom-room w/o a sun
when
you are dreaming graduation is near
gooooo!
goooooooo
gooooooooooo!

when you are dreaming

that is

when you are awake when

French violet flower petals

greet you like van Gogh &

all the streets

lead to

where you are . . .

Klarissa hugged me. started to sing a melody. outta nowhere. totally. everyone in class was applauding. like everything was comin' outta me. for the first time in my life. the sky. the door that Jason Blocker cracked. and the fire that filled. me

& there is nowhere to

go o o o o o o o o o o o o o o o o o o o o o o o
you know you know

down below & high a b o v e

it's all the same
you are singing

{ LUCKY Z.
(aka Luciano Zacarías Flores)
Pacifico Heights School.
Rm. #277 }

For Alyson Day, my editor,
who saw this before I imagined it
For Julie Kline, who heard it before I did
For Kendra Marcus, my agent,
who asked me to be patient
For Margarita,
my partner, who simply knows it
For Lauro Flores,
who believed in me from the start
For Nicole Chang, my niece,
and her husband, Luke, &
their most beautiful children, Jeremy, Hailey,
Anthoney, & Jonathan
For my granddaughter, Rayne
For Victor Martinez, brother, sensei,
For Tom Lutz, for his eye
For Mario Garza, for the fab design draft
For my familia Herrera in Mesquite, N.M.
For my children,
Almasol, Joaquín, Joshua, Marlene & Robert
For Lucky Z.